SHE'S NOT JUST TYRA ANY LONGER

THIS IS A NEW YORK REVIEW BOOK
PUBLISHED BY THE NEW YORK REVIEW OF BOOKS

435 Hudson Street, New York, New York 10014
www.nyrb.com

ISBN 978-1-68137-374-4
Printed in China 10 9 8 7 6 5 4 3 2 1

VIVALDI

HELGE TORVUND AND MARI KANSTAD JOHNSEN

TRANSLATED BY
JEANIE SHATERIAN AND THILO REINHARD

THE NEW YORK REVIEW CHILDREN'S COLLECTION
NEW YORK

A soft scratching sound.
A soft little paw clawing the cardboard.
How happy a sound can make you.
Tyra stays in bed a little longer, feeling how
the scratching sound mingles with daylight.
The light comes in through long yellow curtains.
Inside her it all becomes a soft, shimmering, scratching joy.
Suddenly she can't lie still any longer. Not for another second.
She jumps out of bed, picks up the tiny kitten, and climbs
back into bed with him, even though this is not allowed.
But right now she is not where things are "allowed" or "not allowed."
She is in a place of pure happiness.
Deep inside her kitten's lively, clawing life.
Her soft, sweet, wild, playful kitty.
He's lying quite still now, simply enjoying the down comforter under him.
When Tyra moves her hand, he lunges at her.
Clawing and biting and play-fighting.
He sways his head back and forth.
    "Oh, you're so cute!" says Tyra.
    The kitten turns toward Tyra's voice and looks at
her with the bluest eyes she's ever seen.
All at once, something has changed.
She's not just Tyra any longer.
She's Tyra and the cat.

Mrs. Berg had noticed that they were looking across the hedge at the little kitten leaping around his mother on the lawn.

"It's too bad," Mrs. Berg had said.

"What is?" Tyra's mom had asked.

As usual, Tyra didn't say a thing. She never said anything when they were outside.

"Too bad this one won't get to live," said Mrs. Berg.

All three of them followed the little kitten with their eyes.

"He won't?" said Tyra's mother.

"No. There were three, and I've given two away. And Mr. Berg," she said, and nodded toward the house, "he says that one cat is enough. So he'll probably have to put this one down sometime soon."

As she was saying this, Mrs. Berg caught the little kitten in her arms. His fur was ginger and white. She stroked his head gently before slipping him over the hedge into Tyra's arms. Tyra looked into a pair of keenly alert eyes. The kitten closed them as she stroked him behind the ears.

Very softly, Tyra said, "Kitty, little kitty!"

Tyra's mother looked at the kitten. Then she looked at Tyra. Tyra's eyes were wide open. First Tyra's mother saw that her eyes were filled with fear. Then she saw that they were pleading with her. Tyra's big eyes were pleading to let the little kitten keep his life. A life together with her.

"Maybe we can take him," Tyra's mother said abruptly.

"You can?" Mrs. Berg's voice sounded unusually happy.

Tyra's mother glanced down at Tyra and softly said, "I'll talk to Dad about it."

Tyra looked at the kitten with tears in her eyes.

"It's all right with me," said her mother, "but first I'll have to talk to Dad."

When it was dark in the house that night and everyone was supposed to be asleep, Tyra's father heard Tyra's mother clear her throat. That's when he knew he wouldn't be able to go to sleep quite yet.

"Yes?" he said.

"What?" she said.

"You cleared your throat. Is there something you want to talk about?"

"No. Did I? Oh, yes. As a matter of fact, there is one thing. You remember that before Tyra was born, we had Carl, the parakeet."

"Sure. What about him?"

"Well, it's just that when he died…there'd been such a mess and so much noise and dust that we agreed we'd never have another bird or fish or any other pet."

"Yes, thank goodness," said Tyra's father.

"Hmm," said her mother, and it was quiet for a while.

"Yes?" he asked, a bit impatiently. "What about it?"

"Well…Tyra saw this kitten."

He gave a deep sigh.

"It's Mrs. Berg. She had three kittens, and now she's managed to give away two of them, but the third, well, nobody seems to want him, and she says Mr. Berg is going to put him down. And Tyra really, really wants him."

Tyra's mother shrugged off the mood that had taken hold of her.

"It goes without saying we won't take him if you're against it," she said, "but you know how hard it's been for her at school. Maybe this could do her good?"

Tyra's father gave an even deeper sigh. And didn't say a word.

"I told her it was OK with me," said her mother.

"Sneaky, sneaky!" said her father.

It was quiet for some time. Then Tyra's father leaned over to his wife, gave her a hug, and said, "Of course Tyra will get her kitten!"

Tyra's mother was happy.

"But I don't want any complaining or whining about the smell of cat pee," said her father.

"Oh, no, of course not," her mother answered right away.

And then they went to sleep.

Tyra lay awake in her room, looking at the
long curtains moving gently in the night breeze.
She was thinking about the kitten with her whole body.
Oh, how she wanted him!
But what if Dad said no?
She was absolutely sure he'd say no.
If only he were nice, like Grandma.
She would have said yes for sure.
She was a thousand times sure that Dad would say no.
Lying in bed, she could almost hear the sound of
her father's voice: *No!* he was saying. *No! No! No!*
But then she fell asleep.

And now the kitten was hers. Forever.
And it was summer. Summer vacation.
Tyra could be with her kitten every single
day that came in through the curtains. All day, every day.
She tied a paper ribbon to a string and teased him with it.
The kitten jumped across the grass like a little tiger
and pounced on the paper ribbon.
She kicked a ball across the floor.
The kitten lurked behind the leg of a chair
and leaped forward like a lion.
She simply sat there, watching him while he licked
his paws and washed himself, as cute as
only kittens who wash themselves can be.
But he had to have a name.

"Well," said her mother with a smile. "Have you found
a name for your kitten yet?"

"No," answered Tyra, "not yet."

She wanted his name to be obvious.
Almost as if he had told her himself.
As long as she didn't give him a name, it was as if time stood still.
As if summer vacation would never end, and what she didn't want to
think about would never begin again.

Tyra tried to hear his name.

When they were out in the garden, she stood looking at the kitten. Then she lay down in the warm grass. And listened. As if she wanted to hear what the grass was calling him. She went in among the red-currant bushes and stood completely still. As if she could hear what the bushes were calling her cat. And she looked up at the chickadee in the plum tree, listening to its sharp, clear song. As if she could hear what the chickadee was calling her cat.

"What are you doing?" said her mother, who had come out onto the porch.

"I'm giving him a name," answered Tyra.

"I see," said her mother.

When Tyra returned to the house, her mother shook her head ever so slightly. And one day Tyra was lying in the grass with her cat on her tummy. The cat lay stretched out and purred. All of Tyra was filled with the vibrating sound. Lying there, she closed her eyes and felt that there was no room for a single thought inside her. A purring cat on her tummy, and all her thoughts disappeared. When she opened her eyes, she looked straight up at a cloud.

"Vivaldi!" said the cloud.

And that would be the cat's name: Vivaldi.

Summer was passing. Vivaldi grew big.

He was wild and crazy and darted up onto the back of the chair when Mom was reading the paper. A few giant leaps and he would be all the way on top of the bookcase while Dad was napping on the sofa.

"Take the cat out into the garden, Tyra," said Dad.

And somehow Tyra managed to catch Vivaldi and take him out to play in the garden. They were the best friends in the whole world. Every so often, when he slept in her room, he'd wake her up with a swift attack on her toes. All of a sudden she'd feel two soft paws wrapped around her big toe in the morning. She smiled. The world was smiling. And rubbing its soft fur firmly against her. It was the best way to wake up!

Evenings grew darker across the lawn.
The leaves on the birch tree turned yellow
and a gust of wind blew them down onto the grass.
Tyra felt a dark gnawing in her stomach.
It was time for school to start again.

"Can I take Vivaldi with me when I go to
Grandma's for fall vacation?" Tyra asked one day.

"Hmm, there's an idea," said Mom. "We'll see."

Tyra was actually a good student. That wasn't the problem. As she put her things into her backpack the first Monday of school at the end of August, it was as if everything smelled of blackboard, chalk, and classroom.
It made her feel scared.
All of a sudden, the painful lump in her chest was there again.

Tyra found her desk and entered the place of no words.
When she was at school, she never spoke to anyone.
Once, she had said a few words.
Tyra can feel their stares.
The others don't hide them any longer. Now they look straight at her.
She just looks straight down. But she can feel their stares.
She feels unwell. Queasy.
She looks straight down while the others make a circle around her desk.
Nearly all of them do it.
Except for Petra.
How do they all know to do that?
And why isn't Petra like the others?

The schoolyard is empty.
Tyra walks out of the classroom.
It is October. Some red leaves among all the yellow ones
on the asphalt. Usually there are lots of kids here. How empty the
place seems now. But Tyra likes it.
She feels that the crying inside her can go to sleep now. Like a cat.
When she thinks these thoughts, it's as if she can smell Vivaldi.
She smiles.
She's had her first piano lesson.

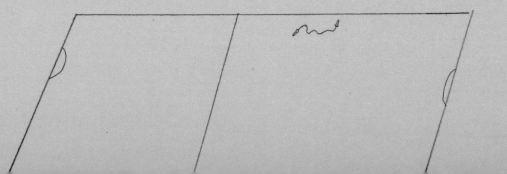

You can cry inside yourself,
and the crying can sleep there
and not wake up. If you're left in peace.
If you get to do what you want and think about what's
happening. But once your thoughts start to race,
that's when things go wrong.
When her thoughts race ahead of her and try to see
what's about to happen. Soon.
Later on.
Behind the next corner of time.
Then the crying inside her wakes up.
And she feels that her eyes are burning.
That her mouth is trembling.
She doesn't want it.
She absolutely doesn't want it to happen.
But it does.

There is singing inside her.
When she watches the rain falling in the puddles.
The round song.
When she sees the evening light in Vivaldi's fur.
The furry light.
The soft song.

Tyra knows about singing and crying.
And she can live with both of them.

An asphalt stare.
A space way too vast.
Like a black hole in her eyes.
Then there are neither songs nor tears.
Then she just wants to run away, fade, disappear.
But her feet are too heavy to move.
And too big.
All the others must be seeing them.
All the others must be hearing them.
And it becomes quiet around her.
A ball lying quietly by itself in the schoolyard
rushes at her and hits her on the shoulder.
That hurt! The ball wanted to hurt her!
She runs. She bolts for the school door.
Like a little mouse.
Her hair streams down her backpack like a tail.
Her heart is pounding.

When she goes to sharpen her
pencil, a bunch of girls are standing around,
looking at pictures in a book.
As she approaches, it's as if
a silent alarm goes off:
They all pull away from her.
They all avoid touching her.
Tyra sees but doesn't understand.
Sees it time after time.
But never understands.

When she practices piano, it's as if the sounds from the keys drive everything else away. It all vanishes. Disappears. She is right here. The sounds feel like silver strings inside her. Vibrating strings. Now and then it doesn't go so well. She gets tired. She wants to get up and play with Vivaldi. But usually she tries once more, and then once more, and finally it turns out right. Tyra and the piano. That's her, too. The singing inside her.

She can feel the hard lump.
It's there when she walks home from school.
There are no words in it.
It's as if it lay inside
a water bubble. When she
touches the bubble, the water
runs from her eyes.

Every so often when she listens
to music, or when she's
alone and dancing,
the lump goes away…almost.
She can dance like a wild thing then.
Feeling the happiness in her legs.
The springiness in her arms.
Feeling that the day is smiling at her.

And every so often when she's
holding the cat in her lap,
and the cat is looking at her,
she feels the lump go away.

And when Mom strokes her hair
after she goes to bed at night.
When Mom just strokes her hair
and doesn't ask any questions or pry.
She doesn't want to say anything.

When Vivaldi is in the room,
things are different for Tyra.
When he curls up in a ball,
asleep in his ginger-red fur,
or when he makes that cozy purring sound,
he spreads peace and music
all around him. Peace music.
She sits down and strokes
his back. He lifts his ears.
Steals a glance with one eye. Looks at her.
It's as if there aren't
any bad thoughts in the world.
His eyes are twinkling at her,
and she forgets.
She has a friend.
A friend who speaks with his eyes.

Tyra and Grandma.
Together at the breakfast table.
The smell of tea.
The taste of orange marmalade.
Autumn leaves. The air is crisp and clear.
A chilly vacation.

Tyra and Grandma together inside the music.
More Vivaldi today. Will they ever get tired of him?
No. Oh, no.
Together they fly into the music.

Tyra and Grandma.
Outside in October. In the light under the big oak tree.
  "I'm probably part tree," says Grandma.
  Typical Grandma, thinks Tyra, to say a thing like that.
  Nonetheless she feels that there's something about Grandma that is
like the tree. Something safe. Something that's been here for a long time.

Even though Tyra had begged her mother, she didn't get to take
Vivaldi along to Grandma's. He had to stay back home
during the break. Mom would feed him
and take care of him.
　"Everyone loves Vivaldi."
　That's Grandma. Typical Grandma.
She plays with the name of the composer and the cat.
Tyra listens to Vivaldi's music.
Summer. He wrote music about all four seasons.
She listens to twittering birds, barking dogs, buzzing
mosquitoes. Gurgling brooks. All of it inside
Vivaldi's music. She looks at a picture of the composer.
He reminds her of something. She also hears someone
crying. And others dancing. She hears storms
building up. And she can picture the still and frozen
winter. Someone skating on the ice.

Tyra flies away. Into the music.
It's light and it's lovely. It's serious and it's sad.
Tyra has listened to Bach and Vivaldi at Grandma's
since she was four. She likes other music too,
but this is the best. Music is like talking without using words.

There must be something wrong with me,
thinks Tyra.
Something I can't see.
Maybe I smell different?
Maybe my back is weird?
Maybe I give off some sort of toxic radiation?
Or maybe it's just that
I feel so sad?
That I never know what to say
when all the others are talking and laughing.

When she's with her cat, nothing goes wrong. Ever.
They play and cuddle and sleep and look at each other.
Well, sometimes something does go wrong. They're playing with a ball of yarn.
It flies over the table and chairs. Tyra holds the end of the string.
Vivaldi pulls and pulls, and suddenly a vase is in the way. It shatters.
   "What was that?" Mom calls from the kitchen.
   Tyra holds her hands over her mouth.
Vivaldi hides under the sofa.
They're completely quiet.
   "Tyyyraaaa?"

One day they do something at school that Tyra likes a lot.
Marianne says that they'll work with clay. Tyra's fingers
feel good. And they get to be with Jon. He's in charge of ceramics.
Everyone gets to make his or her own cup. They can
choose different glazes, and Jon asks what kind they want to use.
Tyra completely forgets herself and starts to speak. Softly she tells
Jon that she wants her mug to be green. But somebody hears her.
Right away, she hears everyone around her start to whisper.

"Mmmug! Mmmmy mmmug!" they mimic her in affected,
mousey voices.

"Mmmmuggg-ah!" Mona squeaks out loud and lets her voice flip
at the end.

"What about you, Mona?" says Jon, pointing at her.

"I want my cup to be blue!" says Mona.

She sneers at Tyra and slowly shakes her head. Everyone laughs.

"Yes, you each get to choose," says Jon.

Then he says very clearly:

"You can each choose whether you want your *mug* to be blue or
green, and whether you want to make the cup with or without a
handle. But to keep it simple, it has to be either blue or green."

Tyra studies the doodles someone has drawn on her desk.
Outside, small snowflakes have begun to swirl down from an icy sky.

Ten degrees!
Vivaldi refuses to go outside. He shakes his paws and hurries inside
again, curling up by the heater.

Tyra hunches her thin shoulders up toward her head as she walks
down the sidewalk on her way to school. She looks at the snowdrifts
stretched out like huge dinosaur bones along the sidewalk. She looks
at the crow on top of a naked, frozen tree. The crow cocks its head
and looks down at Tyra.
   "Hi!" says Tyra softly.
   The crow looks away.
Tyra looks across the field toward the river. Oh! The world is so
white. So clean and new. The cold lump inside her is melting; she's
so happy to see that the world is like new again. What if everything
could begin again, and all the old things be forgotten!

When Tyra gets to the schoolyard, she can feel the stares
without looking up. She can hear the whispering clumps of girls
without listening. Their stares are as sharp as ice-cold winds and their
whispers are like the whispering wind in the willows by the river. Tyra
shivers and tries to rush inside. But suddenly her feet are so heavy.
The schoolyard seems so huge. She has to make it all the way over
there, to the entrance. She lifts one foot, and they all look at it.
They all turn toward her and look at her foot hanging in midair.
Will she be able to put it down without stumbling?
Will she be able to lift her other foot?
Although Tyra hasn't closed her eyes, she has a way of not looking.
She can't bear to look. So she looks without looking.
She closes her eyes while they appear to be open.

Suddenly someone puts a foot in front of her and jerks her foot back. She falls headfirst onto the ice. Waves of girls' laughter flood the schoolyard. At first, Tyra lies quite still. Will she manage to get up again?
Yes, she does. She brushes the snow off her arms.
   "But Tyra, you're bleeding!"
   It's Marianne, the new teacher. She has yard duty.
   "Go away!" hisses Tyra.
   Marianne stares at her in surprise. The other teachers have told her that Tyra never speaks at school. But now she's actually spoken. Marianne sits down and says as softly as possible:
   "Is there anything I can do?"
   Tyra silently shakes her head.
Marianne also shakes her head.

The classroom is extra bright because of all the snow outside the windows.
Everyone is in a good mood. They're going to draw.
Today they have a substitute—the art teacher is sick.
Almost all of them like to draw. Tyra runs her hand across the thick
yellow-white paper in the sketchbook. She feels like drawing something special.
But what? She simply begins, drawing without stopping.
It's as if something is happening inside her and on the paper. She feels a wild
excitement, a joy in each pencil stroke, an almost creepy strength.

As if drawing could be dangerous, in a way?
She keeps on drawing. She draws the stares that rush at her like ice-cold winds.
The foot that shoots out and trips her.
Around and around it goes. Faster and faster.
Suddenly the substitute is leaning over her desk.
Has he been standing there for a long time? He's talking so loud.
As if he'd said her name and she hadn't answered.
    "*Tyra!*"
    "Yes," says Tyra in a low voice and puts down her pencil.
    "What *are* you doing?" he asks.
    Now Tyra can see it. She has drawn dark curlicues across the whole page.
With the tip of her pencil. And she's pressed down so hard that she's made a
hole in the paper, and in the sheet below. Oh, no!
    Now the substitute bends down and leafs through her sketchbook.
    "Let's see," he says gently. "Take the colored pencils and draw a new picture.
Remember what I said: Draw something that has to do with winter, OK? Ice-
skating. A snowman? Can you draw a snowman?"
    Tyra nods, full of shame.

Now she can sense that the others are sending looks to each other.
Eyes that talk to each other.
Maybe they don't want her to see it.
But it could just as well be that they actually *do* want
her to see it. What did they want? What do they want?

Their eyes are saying:
    "She's so out of it!"
    "She's contagious!"
    "Let's stay away from her!"

Their stares shoot into Tyra.
They stick to her soul like cringe stains.
Wherever a cringe stain lands, your soul shrinks. As Tyra's soul
is shrinking, she can feel herself becoming smaller. She can be
standing right there in the classroom and feel herself shrinking.
When she goes to get a book from the bookcase by the teacher's
desk, she's pretty much her usual size. But on the way there and
on the way back, the others shoot so many stares at her that by
the time she returns to her desk, she's so small that it's almost
impossible for her to get into her chair.

But one of them doesn't look at her that way.
Petra.
Petra, who reads so slowly. Who makes so many mistakes.
Sometimes she hangs out with Tyra
during recess. But it's not that easy, because
Tyra never says anything. And usually
someone else comes and wants to be with Petra,
chattering away and whispering into Petra's ear.
Shooting cringe stares at Tyra.
Tyra doesn't say a thing,
so Petra goes off with the others.
Tyra stays behind in her timid world.
A big playground, and a little girl in a green woolen hat.

Tyra's mother always wants to hear how things are going at school.
Then Tyra sometimes enters the place of no words even at home.
She doesn't know what she can say.
She doesn't know what she should say.
She doesn't have anything to say.
She can't find words for the things that are happening.
Mom nags her and asks questions. Falls silent. Looks at Tyra anxiously.
Tyra hears her parents talk about it afterward.
    "Today she was like that again," says her mother.
    "Hmm," says her father.
    Then they talk together in hushed voices.

Talk, talk, talk.

"It's different with you," says Tyra to Vivaldi, and scratches him behind the ears. "You understand everything, without a word."

Suddenly Vivaldi pounces on her and playfully clutches her hand. His hind legs are kicking wildly and he bites her fingertips. Tyra laughs.

"Oh, you're a tough one! And you can put up a fight. But me," she sighs, "I'm good for nothing."

Vivaldi rubs against her.

Tyra runs her hand over his back and looks out the window with sad eyes.

For her birthday Tyra gets
a book from Grandma.
A book about Antonio Vivaldi.
About his life and times.
She reads that he was very famous
because of his music.
That he had red hair.
That he traveled around Europe
performing,
and people were thrilled.

But then they forgot his music,
for over a hundred years.
His music slept for a hundred years.

Then something changed.
And people suddenly heard again
how beautiful his music was.
So strange. Things like that can happen.
Something's there. Then it's gone.
And then it comes back.
Just like the song Tyra learned from Grandma:

First there is a mountain.
Then there is no mountain.
Then there is.

Tyra thinks it's great to live in a time when people
know about Vivaldi.

She puts her finger on the letter *p* in a book.
She puts her finger on the bark of a tree.
She puts her finger on a frosty window pane.
She puts her finger on the bone in the middle of her chest.
She knocks on it three times with her finger.
It makes a slightly hollow sound.

When Tyra sits in a chair, she sits with her legs crossed and
with her one hand on top of her knee. Her other hand points
forward with her thumb up in the air, as if she's about
to shake someone's hand. This way she can feel the air,
the room, and the mood. It feels right to her to
do this when she's in a room.

Just like Vivaldi, who walks around a room and sniffs at
everything.

Sometimes, when she's sitting like that, she remembers
other days. Days that have disappeared but
come sailing back into her memory.

She's walking down the dry road.
Soon it will be fall.
Summer will last a little longer.
She's wearing a light, new dress.
Her mom is walking beside her, holding her hand.
The sun is shining in the leaves and heather.

The schoolyard is all dresses and excitement.

So much happiness in their small backpacks.
So much anticipation in their pencil cases.
So much dread in their little knees.

She looks around.
The schoolyard is so big.
She can't count all the children.
She can't pace out the distance
from the birches at the edge of
the soccer field to the school's front door.

Once they are in the classroom,
her big eyes look straight at the teacher.
Her whole body feels happy. A spotless happiness.
A happiness that lies waiting like the freshly sharpened
colored pencils in her pencil case.

And Tyra remembers more:

The days go by and the other girls
start to clump together,
laughing and having fun.

When she comes near a group
of girls, they stop talking.

And she stays silent.
And no one says anything
to the girl who doesn't say a word.

They can't hear her at all.
She can make herself so small that they
don't see her either.

Or she remembers summer days
at Grandma's:

Tyra lies in the grass and opens her eyes.
She looks at the yellow flowers.
Buttercups and dandelions in the green grass.
She sits and weaves a wreath.
She puts the wreath on her head.
In her white dress
and her yellow crown
she dances her princess dance
through the tall grass.
    "Tyra!"
    That's Grandma calling.
    "Time to eat!"
    "My, you're lovely!" says Grandma,
looking at the wreath.
    Tyra answers with a smile.

Dancing and smiling.
They're good things
that a body can understand.

Marianne lifts the CD player onto her desk and plugs
it in. She puts in a CD and says,

"Now you'll get to hear something great."

She presses Play, and suddenly Tyra is in another world.

It's Vivaldi. It's "Spring"! Tyra takes in the music and remembers its
movement and melody. She remembers its color and joy. Even
here in the classroom she can sense the joy in this music.

"Can anybody tell me what we're listening to?" says Marianne, casting
a brief glance across the class.

Tyra's arm flies up into the air before she knows what she's doing.
When she comes to her senses, she thinks: Yes, I'll answer. I'll talk.
I have something to say! I can answer this question. I want to answer this question!

Marianne looks at the CD case.

Then she says, "Well, I don't suppose anyone knows."

Tyra holds up her arm, stretching it, waving it back and forth.
Look at me! The others see her. But Marianne doesn't. And the others
don't say a word. Some of them shoot cringe stares at her.

Marianne says, "It's Vivaldi. *The Four Seasons*."

Tyra puts her arm down. She sits completely still.
She is trembling inside. She was so excited, so thrilled. Wanted to answer.
But now. Now she's sad, sad and silent once again.
She is so sad that her sadness doesn't end. She's sad that whole period.
And the next period. And she's sad when she goes home.
She dumps her backpack. Goes into her room. Slams the door behind her.
Her mother catches a glimpse of her from the kitchen.
She sighs heavily.

"Does everyone have to go to school?"

Petra is sitting on the terrace with her mother and father in the April sun, a pitcher of juice on the table.

"You know they do," says Petra's father. "Are you having a hard time again? With reading?"

"No, it's not me. It's nothing."

For a moment all is quiet. The Easter lilies sway gently in the cool breeze. A robin is perched on the branch of a small pine tree at the foot of the hill. His red breast is so brilliant.

"Look!" says Petra.

"Yes," says her mother. "He's like our own little bird, that one. He's always here in the garden, or at least it seems that way."

The robin flies off to a birdbath.

"He's tame, all right."

"That's just because I gave him food all winter," says her father. "Who is it, then?" he says to Petra.

"What? No, I said it was nothing."

"But I think something's going on. Someone is having a hard time."

Oh, Dad always reads her thoughts. It's really creepy.

"Am I right?"

Petra looks at him. Her eyes are a little moist. Should she say something?

"Yeah, you're right. It's Tyra. No one wants to be with her. They trip her. And sometimes they kick her too."

"Hmm?" says her father and looks at her calmly.

He has a wrinkle in his forehead.

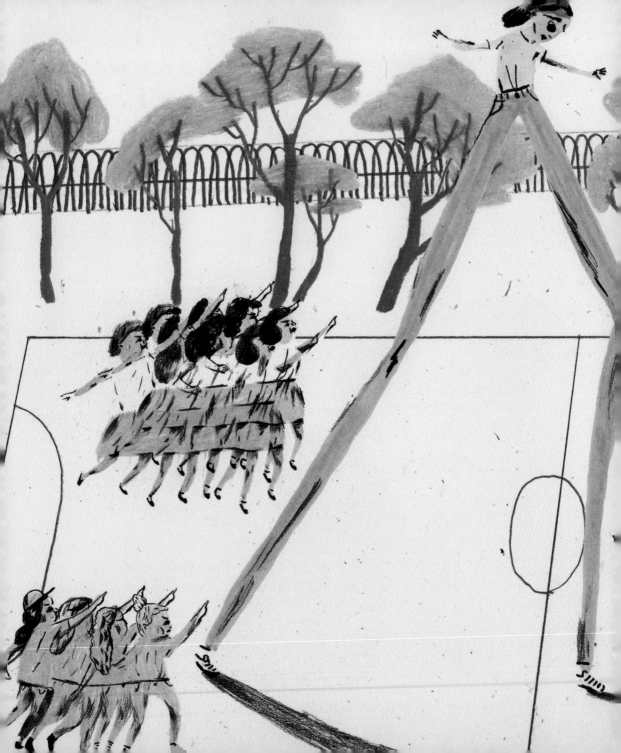

"Is this a recent thing then? Have they just started this?"

"No, it's been going on for a long time," says Petra. "I try to hang out with her, but then…then Anne and Mustafa want me to be with them and they don't want Tyra around. Everyone avoids her. They make a big circle around her."

Her parents look at each other.

"Everyone?" says her mother.

"Yes," says Petra.

"But this has to stop!" says her father.

Petra had hoped that he would say exactly that, but at the same time it was a bit scary. Because what was he going to do?

Would the kids who kick Tyra find out that she was the one who had told on them? Would they kick her too?

Petra's father phones the principal and has a long talk.
The principal phones Tyra's parents and has a long talk.
The principal phones a psychologist and has a long talk.

A few days later Tyra's parents walk into the principal's office.
The principal and the psychologist are already sitting there.
The four of them have a long talk together.

"Tyra, come here," says Tyra's mom one evening.

Mom and Dad seem serious. They look at her. Both of them. At the same time.

"Yes?"

"We've had a talk with the principal," they begin.

Tyra lowers her head and enters the place of no words.

"We talked about how you don't say anything at school. And he told us how your classmates treat you."

But none of the grown-ups know about that! thinks Tyra.

"The principal knows someone who would like to talk to you and try to help you. Would you be willing to talk to him?"

"Is he nice?" asks Tyra.

"Yes, he seems nice," says Mom. "We've talked to him. He's talked with lots of other kids who've had a hard time at school."

"OK," nods Tyra.

"His name is David," says her father. "We'll make an appointment for you if you like."

Tyra goes to find Vivaldi.
She stuffs him into a big empty box on the floor.
Vivaldi looks at her in bewilderment. She closes the lid.
It's completely dark inside.
She can hear him scratching against the cardboard.
He wants to get out.
She pounds her fist against the box.
Vivaldi meows.

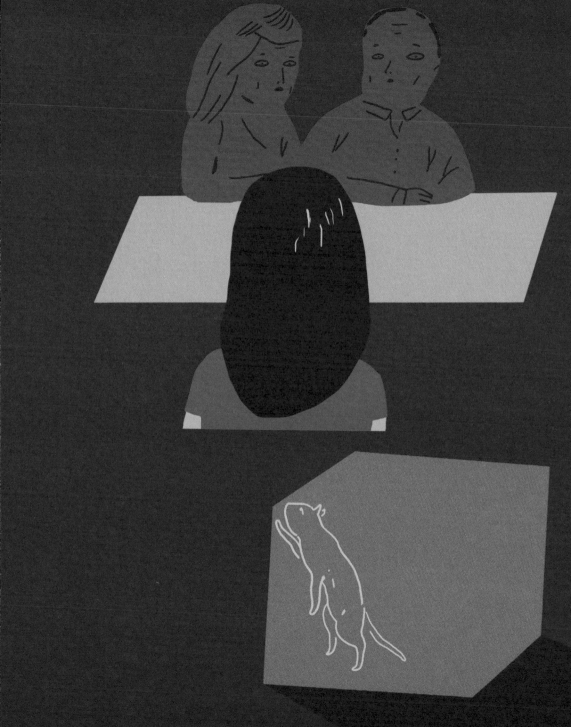

Tyra hurries into the hallway. She's late.
She hangs up her coat between Anna's yellow coat
and Petra's gray coat. Then she goes into the classroom.
Everyone looks up. Most of them quickly look down again
when they see who it is. Petra smiles at her and
nods. But some of them glance at each other
and roll their eyes.

They have math. Tyra gets to work, and things go well. Then it's
time for lunch. They go to the cafeteria. As soon as Tyra gets in line,
the others leave. Aren't they going to have any lunch?
Yup, as soon as she's gotten hers, they get back in line.
When the bell rings and Tyra goes to put on her coat, she sees
that there aren't any coats hanging next to hers.
But aren't Petra and Anna still in the cafeteria? Then she sees
that their coats are hanging four or five pegs away now.
Nothing's hanging next to Tyra's coat.

One day Tyra doesn't go home after school. She goes to David's office for the first time. Marianne takes her. Marianne knocks on the door and opens it.

"Come in!" says a deep and gentle voice.

Marianne steps to the side, and Tyra enters first.

"So you're Tyra," says David, and he shakes her hand.

Tyra nods and looks at him. He looks all right, but she's so tense. She doesn't say a thing.

"Please sit down," says David. "Is it all right if Marianne leaves now?"

Tyra nods.

Then they're alone. Tyra is thinking.

She looks at a picture on one of the cabinet doors. A bear playing the accordion.

Another picture on the wall. A head with wings?

Could there be words for the wordless here?

"I've heard what the principal has said, what Marianne has said, what your parents have said. But now I'd like to hear what *you* have to say. What would you like to talk about?"

Tyra remains silent.
For a long time.
But David doesn't get impatient or irritated or upset.

He just looks at her.
Tyra answers very softly. And she begins with a single word:
  "Vivaldi."

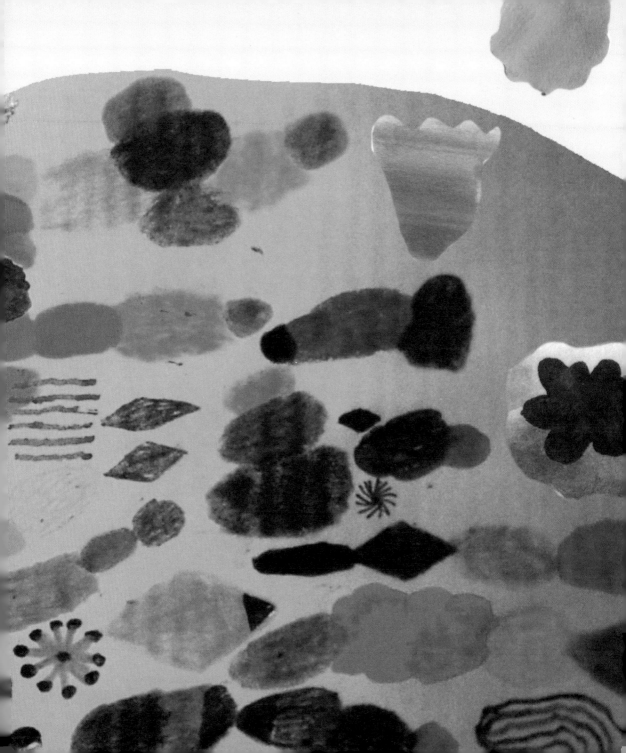

SHE'S TYRA AND THE CAT